"YOU GET AWAY FROM MY KITTY CAT," LUIGI ROARED. "YOU NO EAT UP MY FRIEND."

Willy smiled and wagged his stub tail. Luigi swung the black skillet at his head. In the nick of time, Willy ducked. Luigi raised the skillet again.

Now, Willy was a dog and dogs are dumb—that's a fact. But Willy was no fool. He spun and took off at a dead-out run. Luigi swung the skillet again. Willy tucked his tail.

Willy didn't have much tail. And if the tail was all he tucked, Luigi's black skillet would have creamed Willy's rump. Only Willy not only tucked in his tail, he tucked his whole rear end. The screen, where I clung, began to swing shut. The last I saw of them . . . Willy was running, all hunkered up. . . . Luigi was hot on his heels, swinging that big, heavy black skillet as hard as he could.

BILL WALLACE

UPCHUCK and the ROTTEN WILLY

The Great Escape

SCHOLASTIC INC.
New York Toronto London Auckland Sydney
Mexico City New Delhi Hong Kong Buenos Aires

No part of this publication may be reproduced, stored in a retrieval system, or transmitted in any form or by any means, electronic, mechanical, photocopying, recording, or otherwise, without written permission of the publisher. For information regarding permission, write to Simon & Schuster Books for Young Readers, Simon & Schuster Children's Publishing Division, 1230 Avenue of the Americas, New York, NY 10020.

ISBN 0-439-82087-1

12 11 10 9 8 7 6 5 4 3 2 1   6 7 8 9 10 11/0

Printed in the U.S.A.   40

First Scholastic printing, January 2006

Cover art by David Slonim

To
Keith and Lynn Heck

The Great Escape

CHAPTER 1

Spring has got to be the best!

Winter is cold and nasty. It's fun to play in the snow. Fun to feel the ice crunch beneath my feet or listen to the quiet of a snowfall. But mostly it's just cold and miserable.

Fall is not so bad. It rains a lot in the fall and it's a little sad when the leaves start to change colors and drop from the trees. That's 'cause it means winter is coming.

Then there's summer. Summer would be my second favorite. There's lots of stuff to do then. Summer brings sunshine and warm—only sometimes too warm.

But I love spring!

I glanced up. Above me I could see the green where leaves were budding out. Beneath my feet,

...arting to grow. It smelled fresh and ...lean and new... Birds chirped and fluttered in the ...trees, just now... returning from their nesting places ...in the south. ...My eyes caught every tiny movement as th..., ...hopped and darted about.

Spring was great!

I waited until the car roared past, then looked both ways and jogged across the street. Once safely on the other side, I turned right, trotted to the end of the block, and turned left. A little less than half-way to the alley was a concrete driveway. A big, double, wooden gate stood there. Between the gates was a crack—right down near the bottom.

I stuck my head through. Twisting, I wiggled my shoulders and chest past the boards. Sucked my tummy in and slipped inside the yard.

As usual, my friend was sleeping in. Quiet as could be, I sneaked across the yard. At the doorway I paused. A deep rumbling sound shook the morning air. I peeked in his room. He snored again. The noise was so loud it made the boards vibrate. His eyes were closed tight. Without a sound, I stepped over his legs and took a seat near the far wall.

The corners of my mouth tugged up when I watched him. Then with a sigh I felt them droop to a frown.

Ugly!

I shook my head, trying to chase the thought away. Nope, there was no other word. Just flat ugly.

And smell . . .

I blinked. The odor made my nose crinkle and my eyes flutter again. Outside, the spring morning was fresh and clean. In here . . . well, the stink was almost enough to make my eyes water.

"They're loud and rude and pushy, too. They'd just as soon fight with each other as with us and . . ."

I closed my eyes, trying to chase the words from my mind. I couldn't make them go away, even with my eyes squeezed so tight they made my head hurt.

All my life I'd been taught . . . every friend I had told me the same thing. . . .

"Their noses are too big. They smell, even when they aren't doing anything. They're noisy, especially if you get a group of them together. (And all it takes to make a group is more than one.) They're loud. They're lazy. They spend the whole day laying around and waiting for someone else to take care of them."

Everybody couldn't be wrong—could they?

"They're just not like us." That's what they'd always told me. "We're smart. They aren't. Sneaky and thieving, yes—but not smart. We like someone else to care for us, but we're bright enough and industrious enough to fend for ourselves. They're useless. We work about the house and yard, instead of just lying around, expecting someone else to do it for us. We have nice ears. We're better looking. We don't smell!"

Even the Mama and Daddy had warned me about them. Each morning as I had left the house, they would caution me not to let them get me, or say something like, "Look out for them."

After all that—after all the years of training and listening and warning—how had I ever thought that I could be friends with one of *them*". Why had I even wanted to?

I blinked and looked across the room. A smile tugged at the corners of my mouth and chased the frown away.

Okay . . . he was ugly. So? And maybe his room smelled like a pit, and his breath was enough to eat the hair clear off my head. . . . So what?

He was my friend!

I watched him a moment, then crouched. My muscles tensed. He was on his back and his soft tummy would make the perfect target. I'd fly through the air and land, smack-dab in his middle. In my mind's eye I could almost see him. He'd totally flip out. He'd be so startled . . . rolling, struggling to get to his feet. I squeezed my mouth and nose shut to keep from snickering at the vision.

I crouched lower. I wiggled my rear end. Like steel springs, my legs began to uncoil, launching me at my target. Then . . .

"*RRRROOooff!*"

The roar came from his enormous mouth. It was so loud it flattened my ears and knocked my whiskers against my cheeks. The mouth gaped open like a bottomless cavern. The air, pushed from his massive lungs, almost blew me backward.

The sudden roar scared me. When my legs sprang, I didn't hit his tummy. I went straight up!

My head clunked against the roof.

My eyes crossed.

Even before I hit the ground, my legs were running. It took just two strides to reach the open doorway. Trouble was, I forgot about those huge, clunky feet that were in my way. I tripped.

I went flying through the door and landed smack on my chin. I slid about five feet before my legs got under me again. Out of control, they raced me halfway to the big pecan tree at the side of the yard before I could make them stop. I stood there trembling, panting and gasping for air.

Behind me I could hear the commotion. Eyes tight, I turned.

He was on his back. Legs churning, he flopped from side to side. He laughed so hard . . . well . . . he almost laughed his tail clear off. (And he didn't have that much tail to spare.)

My eyes scrunched down tighter. He rolled back and forth. He laughed and laughed and laughed.

"It's not funny!" I hissed.

That only made him laugh harder. Flat on his back with his head hanging out of the open doorway, he pointed at me.

"You ought to see yourself," he cackled. "Your tail's as big around as your head. You're so puffed up, it's a wonder you didn't explode. I can just see it . . ." He had to stop talking. He was laughing so hard he couldn't catch his breath. "Cat blows up . . . hair flying all over the place. Fur balls fill the air . . ."

"It's not funny!"

Suddenly his face got real serious. Slowly he rolled over to lie on his tummy. His crossed paws dangled from the open door. He frowned. He studied me for a moment, then nodded.

"Yep. You look just as hilarious, right side up, as you did upside down." Then his roaring laugh almost shook the ground beneath my feet.

"That's enough, Rotten Willy. Knock it off."

"Oh, don't get so fuzzed up, Chuck." A sly smile wriggled across his face. "Yeah," he repeated. "Don't get so fuzzed . . . Upchuck."

Then he broke out roaring with laughter.

A puff of red exploded before my eyes. My teeth made a grinding sound inside my head as I gnashed them together. I charged.

I leaped through the open doorway, landed smack on top of his huge, square head, and bit down on his ear as hard as I could.

Bad move!

A tiny squeak came from his huge mouth as he leaped to his feet. Trouble was . . . his room was really small. He was really big. I was on top of his head—between him and the roof.

My head banged against the boards. Only this time instead of crossing my eyes, I saw these sparkly, little twinkling stars. They were kind of pretty. Then everything went black.

CHAPTER 2

My eyes fluttered. I felt cold and wet. I was on my side—but where? Where was I?

Struggling to my feet, I coughed and sputtered. The sound of running water came to my ears. I looked around. So much water streamed from the fur on my left side, it looked like a waterfall. The water streamed down, splashing into a small pond. Made of white plastic, the pond wasn't very deep. It only came about two inches over my paws.

It was Rotten Willy's water bowl.

My wet whiskers sprang up on one side. Disgusted, I looked in the other direction.

Willy stood there. He frowned, making his big, ugly, black face look worried. His soft brown eyes opened wide when he saw me glaring in his direction.

"Are you alive? Are you okay?"

"Sure I'm alive," I sneered at him. "But I'm not okay. I'm wet! I wish you'd quit dropping me in your water dish."

He ducked, kind of scrunching both his head and neck down between his massive shoulder blades. A sheepish smile curled his ugly, floppy lips.

"I'm sorry. I didn't know how else to wake you up . . . Chuck."

"Don't start with me again, Willy," I hissed. "You know how much I hate that nickname."

"I was just teasing, okay? Just playing with you, all right?"

When I didn't answer, he nudged the water bowl with his nose. "Your special person is Katie, right? And she had a boyfriend who didn't like you because Katie named you Chuck, after another boyfriend she had, right?"

I still didn't answer.

"So, you threw up in his convertible and he started calling you Upchuck. I think it's cute. It's nothing for you to get all fuzzed up—" Suddenly he stopped. Snickering to himself, he turned away.

One pounce carried me from the bowl. Water slopped and sprayed in all directions. I stood there, dripping, then shook as hard as I could. It helped some, but all my fur was still plastered against my side.

"I hate it," I hissed. "And I hate being wet, too!"

I licked my side to squeeze some of the water out. "Cat's can't stand being wet. I've told you that."

Willy shrugged his ears.

"Well, it worked. I mean, it saved your life, didn't it?"

I ignored him and kept licking.

"Well, didn't it?"

I stopped to glare at him.

"All right," I said with a sigh. "Last time—when Rocky knocked me off the fence—I guess it saved me. But that was only 'cause Rocky and the two poodles who moved in where Tom used to live kept me stuck in the trees for three days. I was dying of thirst. This time . . ." I started licking again. "This time I wasn't thirsty. I was just a little dazed. All it did was get me wet!"

"Well, it was your own fault." He plopped down on his stub tail.

"My fault?"

"Yeah." He cocked his head to the side. "If you hadn't bit me on the ear—"

"The only reason I bit you," I interrupted, "was because you were laughing your tail off at me, and you called me Upchuck. It made me mad."

"Well, the only reason I was laughing my tail off was 'cause . . ." Suddenly he stopped. I could see a little twinkle in his eye. He turned his enormous, square head away so I couldn't see him laughing.

"Ah, shut up!" I hissed.

That even made him worse. After a moment or two, he quit, took a deep breath, and turned back. "The only reason I barked at you is because you were going to jump on my tummy. If you hadn't planned to scare me first, I never would have scared you. And if I hadn't barked . . ."

Again, his lips clamped shut. The laugh came out of his nose as a loud snort. He turned away, but I could see his sides jiggling in and out.

"Ah, shut up!" I hissed again.

It took him even longer to stop laughing. Finally he trotted over to where I was.

"I'm sorry." It didn't sound all that sincere, 'cause he was still chuckling. "Here, let me help dry you off."

He leaned over. His broad tongue lapped out of his mouth. A little drool dropped from the end when it came toward me.

I spun on him and held up a paw. Claws sprang out.

"Forget it! I'm fine. I can do it myself!"

Rotten Willy went back to his doghouse and curled up. When I finished drying, I felt better. Dry cats have a lot better attitude. The spring sunshine felt warm. I curled into a ball and watched him. My eyes were still tight and a little angry.

Willy and I had been friends for almost four months now. This was our first fight. Maybe dogs and cats really can't be friends.

I used to have normal friends. Louie had been my friend. Louie was an alley cat, only he got smushed by a car. Tom had been my friend, too. Tom was the cat who lived right across the street. Only Tom and his people moved away. My Katie was my friend. She was mine because she was the one who loved me and petted me and let me sleep on her pillow at night. Only My Katie got old. She grew up and went away to a place called college. They had all been good friends. They were normal—cats and people—but Willy . . .

Willy was . . . *a dog!*

As I watched him, I couldn't help remembering how I didn't even know he was a dog—not at first. The animal was so gigantic, I just knew he was a bear or some other kind of strange animal. When my friend Tom had asked what he was—he'd said he was a Rott and he was Willy. Somehow, Tom and I didn't hear it too well, or we got it all confused. Anyway, we thought he said he was a Rott and Willy. When we said it fast, it ended up Rotten Willy. It took us a few weeks to figure out he wasn't really some strange animal called a Rotten Willy, but a Rottweiler dog, and his name was Willy.

We had finally figured it out—right before Tom and his people moved away. When new people had moved into Tom's house, they brought animals. I just knew there were cats in the two cages they put in the garage, so I had waited for them in the pecan tree in their backyard.

But when the people opened the garage door, these two, ugly, nasty, fufu poodles came tearing out. I'd never been so scared in my life. I was stuck in the tree. One limb of that pecan arched out over the neighbor's yard. That was where Rocky lived. Rocky was the meanest Doberman in the world. I had to be really careful when I walked out on that branch to jump to the limb of the other big pecan tree in the Rotten Willy's yard. If I missed the jump, Rocky would eat me for sure. Even if I made it, there was still no place to go. Between the fufu poodles under one tree, the Rotten Willy under the other, and Rocky in the yard between—I was stuck! All I could do was pace back and forth in the trees and wait until I starved to death or died of thirst.

I had been struck there for so long that I was half dead before I tried to make a break for it. Desperate, I tried to walk the board fence between Rocky's yard and Rotten Willy. Only Rocky jumped against the fence and shook me off. I landed in Willy's yard. I knew he was going to eat me. He didn't. Instead, gentle as my mama used to, he picked me up in his enormous mouth and plopped me in his water dish. Then he dried me and kept me from freezing to death during the cold winter night.

*　　*　　*

I looked at him and my tight eyes relaxed. Finally I sighed and walked over to his house. A brown eye peeked at me. He raised his huge head.

"I'm sorry I laughed at you."

I smiled and gave a little shrug. "I'm sorry I bit you on the ear. Does it still hurt?"

He shook his head. "Not bad."

I stepped over his paws. "Here, let me take a look."

He put his head back on the floor. I stretched, but still wasn't tall enough to see. So I climbed up. With my hind feet on his leg, one front paw on his nose, and the other on his neck, I leaned over and licked where I'd hurt my friend.

CHAPTER 3

It's a good thing that dogs don't taste as bad as they smell. I licked and cleaned and cleaned and licked until I was sure his wound was okay. Then I curled up on his back and we took our catnap. I mean dognap. I mean . . . well . . . okay, we took a nap.

Long naps are nice during the winter when it's wet and cold outside. In spring, when the days are warm and pretty, it's a totally different matter. We hadn't napped very long at all when my eyes fluttered open. I was rested and refreshed and ready to go. Willy wiggled and gave a little grunt when I stood to streeetttttch.

I dug my claws in—not enough to hurt him—just right. I started kneading his back.

Cats love to knead. Left, right, left, right, squeeze, relax, left, right—knead, knead, knead.

"Mmmmmm," Willy moaned. "That feels good."

"My claws aren't out too far, are they?" I purred.

"Nope. Just right. Mmmmmm."

A sudden movement caught my eye. I ducked down so I could see through the open doorway. A bird fluttered to the edge of Willy's food bowl. Nervous and twittery, he looked around.

"Don't stop." Willy complained. "I was really starting to enjoy—"

"Shhhhh," I interrupted. "Don't make a sound. Don't move."

I crouched. My tail flipped. My rear end wiggled. If I pounced low and straight instead of up . . . if I hit the ground, only one time, then leaped . . .

The bird grabbed a chunk of food and flew away.

"Darn! Missed him."

"Who?"

"The bird."

Willy raised his head. He kind of leaned to the side. "What bird?"

"Never mind." I sighed. "He just flew away."

Without getting to his feet, Willy gave a hard shake. It was like standing atop an earthquake. The ground moved beneath my feet and I slipped off his side. With a grunt, he got up.

"Want to go chase him?"

"Who?"

"The bird."

"What bird?" I asked, peeking outside the doghouse.

"The bird that flew away."

"No." I curled my tail and sat. "You can't catch 'em after they fly away. Got to sneak up on 'em. Once they get to the trees . . ."

Suddenly I saw one corner of his big, floppy lip tighten to a smile. "Let's play tag." The instant he said it, he clunked me on the head with his enormous paw. "You're it!"

I heard his toenails clack against the floor of his house, then *WHAM!*

Something hit me. It was his rear end, when he charged through the doorway. Willy just brushed me. I doubt that he hardly felt it. But to me, his wide rump struck with such force that it sent me tumbling. I ended up in the corner with my head on the floor and my feet and tail in the air. It was kind of an awkward position. Cats are cool. It's a fact. We're just about the coolest things in the whole animal kingdom—even cooler than people animals. Although they can read and talk with mouth noises instead of smells and twitches, we still got them beat—most of the time. Being stuck on my head in a corner with my butt in the air . . . well . . . it simply was *NOT* cool!

I twisted and scrambled to my feet. My fur jerked and rippled all up and down my body. There was no sound of Rotten Willy laughing. I peeked out

the doorway. None of the mice who lived in the
hole next to the air conditioner squeaked. Not even
the bird bounced up and down and laughed on his
limb in the pecan tree. He was too busy munching
on his stolen chunk of dog food. My tail jerked
from side to side.

You're okay. You're still cool, I told myself with
a sigh. Nobody saw you. Still, just thinking about
it . . .

Being upside down with your tail in the air is a
very undignified position for a cat. We're graceful
and have fantastic coordination. We cats always
land on our feet—not our head. My tail began to
jerk from side to side. Casually, as if nothing had
happened, I strutted out into the yard.

Willy peeked from behind the pecan tree. He was
so huge, his ribs and chest stuck out from one side.
It was like watching a horse trying to hide behind
a sunflower stalk. I wondered if he really thought
he was hidden.

I guess so, because when he saw me look in his
direction, he yanked his head back.

Yeah . . . like I couldn't see the rest of him. . . .

Still cool, I strutted across the yard. I looked all
around, like I was searching for him. And . . . when
I was about two leaps from the tree, I charged.

Willy took off. His big, clunky paws kicked dirt
and grass into the air when he raced from his hiding
place. I jumped. My paw just missed his stub tail.

That's only because at the last second he tucked it against his fat bottom. I hit the ground running. I only chased after him a few feet before I stopped. Although quick and agile like most cats, my legs were just too short to keep up. His fat paws and long legs sped him clear to the far side of the yard before he stopped.

There, he turned to look at me. He had the goofiest, sloppiest grin on his face. "What's wrong?" he taunted. "You must be getting slow in your old age."

I didn't let his insult bother me. Slow and cautious, like easing up on a mouse, I moved toward him. If he started to his right, I took a step to my left. If he moved left, I countered. I was almost close enough. Just another step or two and . . .

The big doof took off again. Head high and the wind flopping his big, loose lips around, he raced beside the fence to the far corner of the yard. I moved in on him again. Once more he took off. This time he hid behind his doghouse.

I'd never seen an animal so big and clunky and dumb! He was so stupid, he probably had no idea that his back was higher than the doghouse. His short, stub tail stuck up like a flag. I felt my eyes roll as I watched it wiggle back and forth.

Instead of coming around the doghouse, like he expected, I waited until I got almost to the door.

Then I leaped to the roof, bounded again, and landed on his back.

"Tag. You're it!" Then I took off before he even knew he'd been got.

I was only halfway across the yard when I heard those thundering paws gaining on me. I ran harder. He was almost on top of me. I darted to the right.

He missed, but he didn't stumble. Instead, he made kind of a circle and closed on me again. I waited until he almost had me, then faked left and dodged right again. Willy slid right past me.

Once more those enormous paws came thundering. I glanced back. Long legs gobbled up the ground as he raced after me. When I looked back at where I was going, my eyes flashed wide. I was headed for the corner. Willy ran faster. I was trapped! I couldn't turn. I couldn't dodge. His massive weight made the ground shake beneath me as he charged.

Suddenly, a thought grabbed me. What if he couldn't stop?

More like a vision, I could almost see it.

Willy was a good friend. He would try to stop. But he was big. Once he got all that weight moving . . . what if he couldn't stop? What if he tried, but . . .

I was a goner! If I got stuck between the enormous dog and the fence, there would be nothing left. I'd end up looking like "roadkill" . . . "freeway pizza" . . . I'd be smushed!

Chapter 4

I ducked.

That was all I could do. I stopped, dead in my tracks and flattened out on the ground. Eyes closed, paws on either side of my head and my belly on the ground, I stuck there as flat as a bug on a fly swatter.

It worked!

Rotten Willy came thundering over me. He managed to tag me with the tip of his nose, but at least I didn't get smushed.

"Tag. You're . . ."

He never got the "it" out. Suddenly there was this horrible CRASH! I glanced up just in time to see Rotten Willy slam into the board fence. He turned his head just in the nick of time. He smacked into the boards instead of the heavy, solid wood post. The fence shook. For an instant Willy kind of scrunched up—all of him squeezed together by the impact. Then he straightened out and shook himself.

Eyes crossed, he looked around.

"Did I get you?"

I nodded. He took off.

Only he didn't take off very far. He wobbled about two steps, then tilted. Staggering sideways, he bumped against the fence. Stood there a moment to get his balance, then he tried again. This time he got about three steps.

"Are you okay?"

"Sure. Fine." He sat down and tried to smile. His head and shoulders kind of went round and round in a big, gentle circle. Inside his head, his eyes rolled round and round in the other direction.

I eased toward him. As hard as he hit, it was a wonder he didn't knock himself out cold. As I got closer, he blinked a couple of times and took off again. I sighed and shook my head. Guess he's all right, I thought. Either his head's so thick, it didn't hurt him all that much, or he's so dumb he doesn't even know he's knocked out.

I gave him enough head start to make sure he was all right, then went after him. We raced round and round the yard until he tried to squeeze between the air conditioner and the house. That slowed him down enough that I nailed his rump with a claw.

He turned and started chasing me.

Playing tag with a Rottweiler is like a cricket playing tag with a steamroller. Sooner or later I was gonna get hurt.

I headed for the pecan tree. Willy was gaining on me. I flattened my ears and whiskers against my head and ran as hard as I could. I jumped.

A huge paw hit my tail. It struck with as much force as the boy people over at the ball diamond used to hit the little, round ball they played with.

Now usually a cat's tail follows the cat. Sometimes it has a mind of its own, though—like if you're really mad, it flips all by itself. If you're really scared, it puffs up all by itself. But most times it just follows along and helps balance.

When Willy hit my tail . . . well, I was in midair, almost to the tree when all of a sudden my tail passed me. I caught sight of it out of my left eye. Then my hind end and the rest of me turned around and started chasing my tail. Claws out, I was ready to cling to the tree and climb out of Willy's reach. Only there was no bark to cling to. I went sailing backward through the air. Paws flailed, claws grabbed, my tail spun—hoping for anything to get hold of. There was nothing.

I missed the tree!

The fence stopped me. My rear end slammed into

it. Upside down, I slid to the ground. I landed on my cheek with my tail stuck up in the air.

Not cool!

Quickly I scrambled to get myself right side up. I fluffed my fur with a couple of quick jerks. Tried to look calm—like I had meant to land on my face with my butt in the air.

Yeah, right.

It didn't work. Above me I could hear birds laughing. I glanced up. A Mockingbird and a Robin stood on two different branches in the pecan tree. They laughed so hard that the limbs bobbed up and down. A little squeaking sound came to my sharp ears. Tight eyes glanced toward the hole in the house beside the air conditioner. As soon as they saw me look in their direction, the three mice scrambled back through the crack to hide behind the brick. I could still hear their squeaking laugh. Above me, the birds squawked and chirped so hard I thought they were going to laugh their feathers off.

Rotten Willy wasn't laughing. He rushed to me and sniffed. The suction from his gigantic nose lifted my fur.

"Are you okay? You're not hurt, are you?"

His big, ugly face looked worried. I tried to smile.

"No, I'm fine. I'm cool."

"Are you sure?"

"Yeah. I knew you were expecting me to jump

for the tree . . . so . . . ah . . . I decided to go for the fence and trick you by landing upside down."

The Mockingbird fell off his limb.

He laughed so hard that he just flipped himself over. Wings fluttering, he managed to grab hold of a lower limb. Still laughing, he had to use his beak to pull himself up.

"You ever see such a clumsy cat?" he called to the Robin. "Did you ever see a cat miss a whole tree before?"

The Robin's laughter bounced his limb so hard I thought it was going to snap.

"Not only does he miss a whole tree," the Robin chirped, "he lies about it, too."

My eyes were hot enough to glow in the dark.

"That's it," I snarled. "You're cat food."

Claws ripped into the bark as I tore up the tree. Like a streak of lightning, I chased after the Robin. He let out a startled chirp and flew off. Last glimpse I got, he was flapping so hard he was probably over the football field before he slowed down. Then I turned on the Mockingbird.

Mockingbirds don't scare as easily as Robins. They have kind of a nasty disposition—especially in the spring when they're protecting their babies. I've even had 'em peck me on the back for doing nothing more than walking across my own yard. This guy gave a little squawk, but he only flew to the end of the limb. There, he turned and laughed at me even louder than before.

I started after him when all of a sudden . . .

WHAM!

The loud noise startled me. My tail jerked—hard. When it did, it lifted my back feet off the branch. I managed to hang on with my front claws, but my rear and my tail hung down.

WHAM!

Wide eyes focused on the sound. It was Rocky! He slammed against the fence. He leaped as hard as he could. White fangs slashed, no more than a whisker's width from my tail.

CHAPTER 5

Muscles in my back tightened. Hard as I could, I swung to the side, trying to get hold of the branch with my hind foot.

I missed.

WHAM!

Rocky leaped again. His fierce jaws snapped. I barely managed to jerk my tail out of the way. Frantic, I struggled to reach the limb and pull myself up.

"I've got you . . . now!" He leaped and barked his threats. "I knew you'd . . . mess up, sooner . . . or later and . . . when you did . . . I'd be . . . ready. . . ."

Rocky couldn't jump and bark at the same time. So every time he was in the air, he managed only part of what he was trying to say. Fact was, I don't think Rocky could even think in complete sentences—much less say something all together.

With all my strength I pulled until my chin was resting on the limb. Then I swung my hind leg.

"I'm gonna get . . . that tail and . . . yank you down from . . . that tree. I'm gonna chew . . . you up into . . . tiny pieces . . . and . . ."

I made it. As soon as all four feet were on the branch, I scampered back to where I was safe. I stood there, panting and watching.

"Are you okay?" Rotten Willy woofed from below.

"Yeah," I gasped. "I got mad at that stupid bird and wasn't paying attention. You talk about dumb. If I hadn't grabbed on to that—"

"Come back, you . . . cowardly cat . . . I dare you . . . to walk back . . . out on that . . . limb. . . ."

I stood at the base of the branch, where it joined Willy's pecan tree. Every time Rocky leaped and barked, all I could see of him over the fence was his pointy nose and pointy ears and pointed head.

"I'm stronger, now . . . and I can jump . . . higher. And . . . if you weren't . . . such a chicken . . . cat, you'd . . ."

"Man, that is one nasty dog," Willy snorted, glaring at the wood fence. "It's dudes like him that give all us dogs a bad name."

I curled my tail and sat down. My fur was just now starting to unpuff.

"I thought you were the only nice dog there was."

Willy shook his head.

"No. A lot of dogs are nice. Most of us won't even bother a cat unless you run from us. Ones like me, who grew up with cats, we don't chase them at all."

"If I could . . . just get my . . . paws on top . . . of this fence . . . I'd climb over . . . there and grind . . . you into dog . . . food. I'd—"

"Ah, *SHUT UP!!!*"

My eyes flashed. It startled me to hear Willy's bark and my hiss say the same thing to Rocky at the exact same instant. We looked at each other and laughed.

"The way I got it figured," I told Willy as I backed down the tree, "it has to be the breed. I mean, Dobermans are pretty big dogs. But you got this big dog with pointed ears, a pointed nose, and a teeny, tiny head. Big dog—tiny head. There's not room for much of a brain inside that ittsy-bittsy skull."

Willy shrugged his ears.

"Might be part of it. But I've met some nice Dobermans in my day. I figure it was more the way his people raised him."

"Come back . . . cat . . . I'll play tag . . . with you . . . just get on . . . this side of . . . the fence and . . ."

Willy and I ignored him. We trotted to his doghouse and lay down for another nap.

"You really think it was his people?"

Willy nodded.

"Yep. His people wanted Rocky to be a watchdog, so they were real mean to him when he was a puppy. They poked him with sticks and scared him and stuff like that."

"How terrible."

Willy nodded his agreement.

"They wanted him to bark and be mean, like them. It worked, too. Rocky won't let people near the house. Not even little kids. He doesn't like cats. I tried to make friends with him. He doesn't like dogs. He's not happy with his people. Fact is, I don't even think Rocky likes Rocky all that much. It's a shame."

I curled up against his tummy and closed my eyes. Trouble was, my eyes wouldn't stay shut. The afternoon was warm and comfortable. I got up, made two circles, then lay down again. Rocky finally quieted. I yawned and forced my eyes tight. There was a breeze, but just enough to keep the air moving—not so much that it tickled my fur or irritated me. I clamped my eyes tighter. There were no birds chirping in the trees. Everything was quiet and peaceful. Perfect weather and time of day for a nap. I flipped one way, then the other. Willy moaned when I got up. Still trying to get comfortable, I made two more circles and lay back down.

My tail wrapped over my face. Then an eye popped open and peeked out from underneath it.

It was no use. No matter how hard I tried, I simply couldn't sleep.

Careful not to wake my friend, I crept through the door and climbed the pecan tree. From up high I could see my whole world.

Behind Willy's fence there was the baseball field, and beyond that, the football stadium. In the fall no one came to the baseball field. Well, maybe now and then a man came to mow the grass or rake the sand. Tom and I used to run across the empty field and sit on the big, wood fence and tease the dogs. I climbed a little higher.

It was still early in the afternoon, but there were already people walking their dogs around the track at the edge of the football field. The lady who lived on the other side of Rocky's house—where my friend Tom used to live—was already there with her poodles. I could see their little, prissy, fufu haircuts even from this far away. To the right was a row of houses. There were no pets in their yards, though. And beyond the houses was Luigi's Italian Restaurant and the busy street where my friend Louie got smushed.

Even higher in the tree I could see over Willy's house. My house was sort of across the street there. Behind it was an empty field, Farmer McVee's place, and . . .

"You're bored, aren't you?"

The unexpected voice made my whiskers jerk. I blinked and looked down. Willy stood at the base of the tree. I frowned.

"I'm not a board. I'm a cat."

Willy smiled and shook his head.

"I didn't say you were *A* board. I said you were bored."

"What's that?" I asked, backing down the tree to sit with him in the lawn.

"It's a people word," he explained. "Like a feeling kind of thing you get. My David used to get it sometimes, when he didn't have anything to do. He'd get that look in his eye—just like the look you had—then he'd say, 'I'm bored.' "

"So, what did he do about it?"

"Well." Willy shrugged his ears. "Let me tell you."

CHAPTER 6

Yeah, right!" I flipped my tail. "I can just see me riding a skateboard, or taking you for a walk on the beach so I can flirt with the girl people. I don't even know what a beach is."

"It's a big, sandy place near the ocean."

"What's an ocean?"

Willy shrugged his ears.

"It's water. It's big. Only you can't drink it."

I shook my head and strolled back to climb the pecan tree. "What good is water if you can't drink it."

"Well," Willy called after me. "You asked what my David boy did when he got bored—so I told you."

At the base of the tree I stopped. Instead of climbing, I rubbed against it to scratch the itch on my side. "I still don't know what bored is. How can I keep from getting something when I don't even know what the something is I got?"

His big mouth flopped open. He looked at me. He frowned and tilted his head from side to side.

"Huh? What did you just say?"

"I said . . ." My tail flipped—a couple of quick jerks. "I said . . . I don't know what I said. I just don't understand bored."

With a sigh Willy sat down.

"Okay, cat," he began. "It's kind of like this. People animals and cat animals are used to doing things. But when they do the same thing all the time, they get tired of it and want to do new stuff. They like to explore and meet new friends and find new places and—"

"You said people animals and cat animals," I interrupted. "Don't dogs like to explore and meet new friends?"

Willy plopped down on his stub tail.

"Well, sure, but we don't usually get to."

"Why?"

"Well, when we're puppies, our people play with us a lot. Only when we get old, they kind of forget about us. They don't play with us or take us on walks. Dogs get used to being bored." He glanced at me. "That's why it's hard to explain."

"So what do you do when you get bored?"

Willy shrugged his ears and his big shoulders,

both. "If I get bored, I just stay bored. I'm used to it."

The fur on my back rippled. "What do other dogs do?"

"Some dogs dig when they don't have anything to do. Other dogs bark. A few chase their tails. No matter what you do, you get in trouble. Best thing to do is just sit around and get used to it."

I tilted my head, way to the side. Looked at him out of one eye. "Why don't you do something?"

"Like what?"

"Well, like go for a walk or go explore. We could even go to Luigi's Italian Restaurant. He fixes the greatest spaghetti and meatballs and—"

"Just how am I supposed to do that?"

"Well, we could climb up in the tree. See that big branch? I'm not big enough to jump from it and get over the fence, but as big as you are you could probably hop from there and—"

There was a loud growling sound when Willy cleared his throat. "I beg your pardon."

"Huh?"

"I think you might have forgotten, but I'm a dog." He held out a paw and wiggled his short, blunt claws at me. "We don't climb trees or *hop*. Remember?"

"Oh, yeah." I shrugged and tucked my tail. "I forgot."

His enormous chest heaved a sigh. "You're bored.

You're a cat. You're not stuck here like me—a dog. Go explore or go eat spaghetti and meatballs with Luigi. I'll be here when you come back. I'll still be your friend."

I sat there a moment, thinking it over. I did need to do something, to go someplace. There just had to be more to life than taking catnaps. Playing chase with a Rottweiler was too dangerous to be much fun. But being alone . . . going places by myself or seeing new things without someone else to share it with . . . It just wasn't the same. It wasn't fun.

Suddenly my whiskers sprang up. I was bored. Willy was bored. We were friends. So . . .

"Come on!" I called with a jerk of my head. "Follow me."

Willy was right behind me when I raced to the back fence. I felt around with my paws. The whiskers on both sides of my face sprang up when I found a soft spot. I started to dig. I dug and clawed the ground. Grass and dirt flew between my hind legs. Willy just sat there, watching.

"What are you lookin' at?"

"You," he answered. "I never saw a cat dig under a fence before."

"Well, don't just sit there. Help me."

"No."

I frowned at him. "Why not?"

His big head ducked low. "I get in trouble for

digging under the fence. The Mama people will get mad at me and call me 'bad dog.' "

I looked around. There was a big shrub in the corner of Willy's yard. I raced to it. Squeezing between it and the fence, I started digging again.

"Now what?" he asked, coming to join me.

"We'll dig here," I said. "We'll dig a hole behind this shrub. Your Mama won't be able to see the dirt. The leaves will hide it." Hard and fast as I could, I began to dig.

"Chuck."

I dug harder.

"Chuck!"

"What?"

Again he sat down. "Can you see how big I am?"

"Yeah. So?"

"So, I'd have to move a mountain of dirt to get under the fence. There would be so much dirt, it would be higher than the bush. There's no way she'd miss it."

My hind end sank to the ground. My tail stuck straight out. It didn't even flip. I sat for a long time, thinking. Finally a smile tugged my whiskers.

"Come on."

Willy followed me to the other corner of his backyard. I sat for a moment, studying the fence. It was what the Mama and the Daddy people called a "privacy fence." I knew the name because they had talked about building a "privacy fence" around our yard. I guess it was called that because the up-and-down boards were so close together that no one could see through—so it made it private. But the boards just couldn't stand there by themselves. The up-and-down boards were about as wide as Willy's head, but only as thick as one of my paws. They were nailed to big pieces of wood, about as wide as both my paws put together. There were two of these boards that ran level with the ground. One was about as high as my ears, the other was up near the top. Every six feet or so these were nailed to big, heavy posts that stuck into the ground. They held the whole fence up.

"What are we doing?" Willy asked.

"We're gonna climb the fence."

"No way!" he scoffed. "I can't climb that."

"Have you ever tried?"

"No, but—"

"Well, at least try. Come on. Stand on your hind feet, right here in the corner. Okay, reach up with your front paws as high as you can. See the big piece of wood, where your nose almost touches? Now, see the other big boards that run level with the ground?"

It was amazing how big he was. With his hind feet on the ground, his front paws almost touched the big board near the top of the fence.

"Now put your hind feet on the bottom rail. The one the fence boards are nailed to."

Willy lifted his hind foot. He peeked under his armpit, but he was so close that he couldn't see. So I helped guide his foot to the board with my paw. "Okay. Now the other foot."

He gave a little hop. His paw reached for the board about three times before he finally got his foot on it.

"Great!" I stood on my hind feet with my front paws on his enormous rump. "Now see if you can get hold of the board and pull. . . . " I helped him. With my paws on his hind end, I shoved. "Get hold of the board and pull yourself."—I pushed—"up. See if you can grab."—I lifted, strained, shoved— "the top of the fence and drag."—I pushed so hard I thought my eyes were going to pop out—"yourself up on the fence. Just a little more. You almost got . . . it . . . Now . . ."

Willy slipped.

CHAPTER 7

The whole world was wet and cold. I blinked. Struggled to force my eyes open. They fluttered.

I was on my side—but where? Where was I? What happened?

I remembered standing under Willy and trying to push him higher on the fence. I remembered his feet scraping on the boards, trying to help me lift. I was right under him when he slipped and . . .

Struggling to my feet, I coughed and sputtered. The sound of running water came to my ears. I looked around. So much of it dripped from my side, it looked like a waterfall. The water streamed down, splashing in a small pond. Made of white plastic, the pond wasn't very deep. It only came about two inches over my paws.

Yep. It was Rotten Willy's water bowl.

I sprang from the water. It sloshed and sprayed around me, the little droplets going in all directions as I leaped.

"Man! I don't believe this. Not again!"

The worried frown left Willy's face and he smiled.

"You're alive!" he yelped. "When I fell, I thought I killed you. You were hardly breathing. I was afraid—"

"Willy?"

"Yes, Chuck?"

"If you don't quit plopping me in your stupid water bowl . . ."

I didn't bother trying to finish. I didn't bother shaking. I didn't even bother trying to dry my fur with my tongue. Dripping, I sloshed across the yard, squeezed through the crack at the bottom of the gate. A trail of water followed me all the way to the edge of the concrete.

Having a Rottweiler land on me was like . . . well, it was like . . . well, I didn't know what it was like. Nothing had ever happened to me that was bad enough to compare it to. I hurt all over. My head throbbed. My legs ached. My back felt like a pop can that the Mama squashed before she put it in the trash—like it had just been all crumpled together and my tail was about five inches closer to my head than where it used to be.

I arched my back about three or four times, to

try and get some of the kinks out. I could hear the crack and pop inside my head. Still stiff and aching, I sat and began to dry my fur.

The hair on my chest and tummy was sopping. I could feel the wet on my back and the top of my head. But there was hardly any water left to drip from my sides. Frowning, I stared back at the path I left on the concrete.

Near the edge where I sat, there were just a few drops of water. But right under the gate, where I squeezed through, there was a regular lake. I frowned, studying it for a moment. Suddenly my eyes flashed and a smile made my whiskers wiggle.

"Willy. Willy," I meowed. "Come here. Quick."

I stuck my head into the crack between the two big wooden gates. Like always, my whiskers flattened against my cheeks. Our whiskers are the way us cats can tell if we can fit through something. If our whiskers can make it through a hole or a crack, the rest of us can get through. My whiskers didn't fit through this crack. Still, for the past four months this is the way I came and went from Willy's yard.

"What is it, Chuck?" Willy woofed. "Is something wrong? Are you hurt?"

"No. Look."

I stuck my head through the crack. Then I pulled it back out again. Then I poked it in once more.

He frowned.

"Watch." I told him. I shoved, turned sideways, and wiggled my way through the gate. Once in Willy's yard, I spun around and squeezed my way back outside. I turned again, stuck my head in, and smiled. "See?"

Now, I've always heard that dogs were dumb. It's just a fact of life. But the look on Willy's face . . . He didn't frown. He didn't smile. He didn't look confused or curious or . . . well . . . it was the blankest look I ever saw in my life. *He just looked.*

"Don't watch me. Watch the gate." I tapped it with my paw. "Watch the one on this side."

Again, I went out and came back. This time Willy smiled.

"It moved."

"Right!"

I was so proud of the dumb mutt, I could hardly stand it. I rubbed against his legs and purred. The ground shook beneath my feet when he plopped down on his rump. I watched as he studied the big, wooden gates. Tilting his head one way, then the other, he looked it up and down for a long, long time. Finally he smiled.

"Thumb bolt's broken off."

"Huh?" I frowned.

"Thumb bolt," he repeated. "One at the base of the right gate. It's gone."

I blinked a couple of times, then shook my head. "The what . . . what's broken?"

"See that metal thing near the top of the gate?" He pointed with his nose. "It's what the people animals call a thumb bolt."

When he saw the expression on my face, he kind of rolled his eyes. "Okay. The big toe on the people animal's front paw is what they call their thumb. They use their big toe, or thumb, to do lots of stuff. A bolt is that long, solid, metal thing. See how it fits inside the hollow metal pieces? Well, people animals use their thumb to slide the bolt one way to open it—then they use their thumb to slide it the other way to lock it. Thumb bolt. Get it?"

Even sitting down, Willy was so tall, he was way above my head. What he was saying was way above my head, too. I kind of shrugged and shot him one of my helpless looks. Willy sighed.

"Never mind. See this thing?" He reached around my left side and jiggled a little metal rod with his paw. "See how it fits down into the concrete? That holds the bottom of the gate so it won't open or jiggle around in the wind. Now, look over here." He reached around my right side and tapped the wood. "See those four holes? That's where the other thumb bolt is supposed to be. But it's fallen off."

He studied the gate for a moment—kind of nibbled on his bottom lip. He began talking to himself.

"Okay . . . the gate's about six feet high and about five feet wide. But the latch is probably only five feet off the ground, so that cuts the angle down a bit. My shoulders are my widest part. Probably twelve inches across. The gate's a rectangle, so that gives us right angles or an isosceles triangle. The square of the hypotenuse is equal to the sum of the squares of the other two sides, so . . . oh, wait. No, that won't work. I'm thinking plane. This is solid geometry. My shoulders aren't flat on the ground, they're about twenty-four inches up. Okay. What was that formula for figuring the base diameter of a cone? Let's see . . ."

"Willy? What *are* you doing?"

"Geometry."

"What?"

"My David used to do his math homework on the bed. I'd lay down and help him. But . . . well, I was a lot better at plane geometry than solid geometry. I can't remember how to find the area of a cone."

My head cocked so far to the side I almost fell over.

"Why are you trying to do that?"

"You don't want me to get stuck, do you?"

My yellow eyes got so tight I could hardly see. All I wanted to do was go eat spaghetti and meatballs. And here's Willy—dumb as a dog one minute, then trying to do some high-level math problem in his head the next. I couldn't decide whether he was a total idiot or some weird kind of a genius.

"Stick your nose through the crack."

"Huh?"

"Your nose." I pointed with a paw. "Push it in the crack."

"How's that?" he asked. His voice was kind of high and whiny, like somebody was pinching his nose.

"Great," I encouraged. "Now shove your head through."

The wooden gate moaned and creaked.

"Now what?"

"You're doing great. Just keep going."

Willy got to his shoulders, then stopped. His claws made a scratching sound as he dug the ground. Pushing, shoving, straining, he couldn't quite force the gate wide enough to slip his broad shoulders through.

I stood up and pushed on his rump with both paws. He tried harder. His muscles rippled. His feet began to spin on the concrete. I stepped back. I raised a paw. Claws sprang out.

CHAPTER 8

That hurt!"

Willy sat on one cheek. He had to bend himself almost double to reach around and lick the other cheek where I'd swatted him.

"Why did you go and stab me in the butt?" he whined.

"You're my friend." I shrugged. "You were stuck. I couldn't just leave my friend stuck there in the gate."

"It hurt!" he complained.

"It worked, didn't it?"

His bottom lip stuck out. "It still hurt."

I smiled and gave him a big, rough, cat tongue kiss right above his eye.

"Quit being such a baby. We're out. We're free. Come on. You're gonna love Luigi."

At the corner we looked both ways and trotted across the street. Willy wanted to see my house first, so we took a little detour to the right. We circled the house about three times. He sniffed at everything. He told me about the squirrels who visited and had pecans buried in the Mama's petunias. He told me that the Mama and the Daddy were happy people and that they liked me, but they also missed My Katie. He told me that the Daddy worked at a place where there were lots and lots of people, but no dogs or cats.

"You can tell all that stuff just by sniffing?"

Willy nodded. "Dogs can tell a lot from smells. Like the place where the Mama works—there are a lot of little kids there. They all have their own separate smells. The smells get on the Mama's shoes and clothes, then she brings them home with her. Most of the kids she is around are happy, but she has one little boy who is very sad."

"The Mama teaches school," I told him. "She likes her class, but I've heard her talk about a little boy named Sam. She says that his mama and daddy are real mean to him and hurt him. But I can't tell all that by smelling."

Willy frowned. "I thought cats had a good sense of smell."

"We do." I nodded. "But not as good as dogs, I guess. Our ears and eyes tell us just as much, if not more."

"It's our noses that tell us stuff," Willy said. "Like food." He stuck his nose up in the air and sniffed. "It's coming from that direction."

"That's Luigi's." I bumped him with my shoulder. "Come on."

While we walked to Luigi's, I asked him about that geometry stuff he was doing. Willy told me that he came to live with his David boy when David was in eighth grade. He was supposed to have learned his math stuff, like multiplication facts, in fourth grade—only he hadn't. "My David kind of cheated, I guess," Willy confessed. "He used to count on his fingers and he was real fast and real sneaky about it." But Willy told me how the Mama had figured it out and made his David learn. She got him these things called flash cards. Willy couldn't read the numbers, but his David would say them out loud—like five times six equals thirty. Then he'd flip the card over and smile when he got the right answer.

Over and over and over again; day and night; at the supper table; while they were watching the noisy box; even before they went to bed—he worked on his multiplication numbers. Willy told me that after he'd heard the stuff about a million times, he started remembering it, too. When his boy got in high school, Willy didn't like algebra. That was because his David was quiet when he did that. But when it came to geometry, Willy's boy used to lay on the bed. He'd say the problems out loud and draw lines and angles and stuff on his paper while Willy watched. Then he'd explain all the rules and problems.

"I don't think My David really believed that I understood him," Willy admitted. "He was just talking to help *him* remember. But I learned them, too."

"I can't believe you can do people math." I glanced over my shoulder at him and shook my head. "That's like big-time stuff."

"I can't." Willy smiled. He followed a pace or two behind me. "Not really. All I can do is what I call mouth math—the stuff My David said out loud. Anything with paper and pencil . . . shoot . . . I can't read a lick. I can't even understand that big sign up there."

I stopped and turned to see what his nose was pointing at. A sneaky smile curled my lips.

"I can read it," I bragged. "It says, Luigi's Italian Restaurant."

Willy's mouth flopped so wide, I thought he was going to trip over his bottom lip. Before he had a chance to figure it out or find another sign to quiz me on to see if I really could read, I took off.

"Come on," I called. "Back door. Follow me."

Luigi was no place in sight. I walked to the screen and rubbed against it. Nothing happened. I meowed. Willy spotted the two big trash cans beside us. He jumped up and put his paws on the edge and peeked inside.

"Oh, man, look at this!" His stub tail wagged so hard it was a wonder it didn't knock his hind feet from under him. "There's some really neat stuff in here. It smells great and—"

"Forget the trash," I meowed. "You eat at Luigi's—you go first class, all the way. Come on over here."

Inside, I could hear pots and pans clattering around. I meowed. Footsteps clicked on the floor, but they didn't come this direction. I meowed louder. Luigi started singing to himself. I jumped up on the back screen, like Tom used to do, and shook it.

A big, round face peeked from behind the corner. The long, droopy, black whiskers under his nose sprang to a smile.

"There's my kitty-cat friends." His rolling laugh almost shook the screen where I clung. "I not see you guys all winter. Think maybe you forget about Luigi. How you live all winter without Luigi's wonderful spaghetti and . . ."

Luigi's eyes popped as big around as some of the tomato paste stains on his white apron. I was just about to turn and hop down so Luigi could open the screen when his big paw slammed against the door. All of a sudden the screen and I were flying backward. When I hit the wall, my nose and

tummy and . . . well, all of me squashed into the screen.

Luigi burst from the open door. He held a big, black skillet in his paw. He raised it above his head.

"You get away from my kitty cat!" he roared. "You no eat up my friend."

Willy smiled and wagged his stub tail. Luigi swung the black skillet at his head. In the nick of time Willy ducked. Luigi raised the skillet again.

Now, Willy was a dog and dogs are dumb—that's a fact. But Willy was no fool. He spun and took off at a dead out run. Luigi swung the skillet again. Willy tucked his tail.

Willy didn't have much tail. And if the tail was all he tucked, Luigi's black skillet would have creamed Willy's rump. Only Willy not only tucked his tail, he tucked his whole rear end. The screen, where I clung, began to swing shut. The last I saw of them . . . Willy was running, all hunkered up. His rear end was tucked so tight, it was almost under his belly when he ran. Luigi was hot on his heels, swinging that big, heavy black skillet as hard as he could.

CHAPTER 9

Our whiskers are really important to us cats. They're suppose to be straight and well groomed. The way the whiskers on the left side of my face got smushed against the screen . . . well . . . they were crinkled up like a wad of paper. Curled and kinky as springs, the whiskers wouldn't straighten out. It threw my whole world off balance.

Willy saw me coming. He peeked from behind a telephone pole at the far side of the parking lot. He was so big, he stuck out on both sides.

"You really think you're hidden?"

"That guy tried to kill me!" Willy panted, leaning out a little farther. "Is he gone? Did he go back inside?"

"He's gone," I said. Out of the corner of one eye, I could see my crinkled whiskers. I wiggled them.

They still wouldn't straighten. So I turned my attention back to Willy. "Would you get out from behind that post. You look like a total idiot."

"I'm hiding."

"You're not hiding." I sighed. "You stick out on both sides of the thing. Come here."

"No."

"Come here!" I stomped my paw. "Now!"

Sheepishly the huge beast eased from his hiding place behind the telephone pole. Looking all around, he crept slowly to me.

"Let's go home. That guy scared me." Willy sat down and ducked his head. "He tried to bash my bottom."

I smoothed at my crinkled whiskers with a paw.

"It was just a simple misunderstanding, Willy. He thought you were going to eat me or something. We'll straighten him out. Come on."

"No way."

Still messing with my kinky whiskers, I only went a few steps when I turned.

"Willy, come on."

"No. I don't even like spaghetti and meatballs."

"You've never had spaghetti and meatballs."

"I don't care. I still don't like 'em. I want to go home."

"WILLY!"

I meowed, then jumped up and shook the screen. I didn't stay there for long, though. All I needed was to have Luigi sling the door open again and get the whiskers on the other side of my face smashed. I just rattled the screen and hopped down.

Willy stood at the far edge of the building. He leaned forward and peeked around the corner. All I could see of him was his huge, square head.

Luigi opened the door. He still had the skillet in his hand. After looking all around, he smiled and leaned down to pet me.

"There's a good kitty cat. Luigi save you. You come to eat good food, not make good food for some big, nasty dog. Luigi fix you big plate of . . ."

With my tail straight in the air and curved at the very tip like a question mark, I trotted toward Willy. Meowing as loud as I could, all the way, I told him to come out from behind the corner. He did.

When Luigi saw him, he raised the skillet above his head. I rushed straight to Willy. Still meowing, I worked in and out between his front legs. I purred and rubbed and weaved round and round. From the corner of my eye, I saw the black skillet come down to Luigi's shoulder.

"Lean over," I meowed.

Willy bent down. I purred and rubbed against his cheek. Luigi's neck kind of stretched up. His head tilted to the side. With my tongue, I kissed Willy on his cheek, then above his eyes and finally on his big, pointed, wobbly ears.

I sure hoped the spaghetti and meatballs would help get the nasty "dog" taste out of my mouth.

It worked!

The black skillet dangled at the end of Luigi's limp arm. He shook his head, then took a couple of steps toward us.

"Follow me," I told Willy. "And wag your tail. Act happy.

When I brought Willy closer, Luigi squatted down and set the skillet beside him. Cautiously he reached out a trembling hand. Willy licked it. Luigi began scratching Willy behind his ears. I guess Willy really liked people animals. His tail was wagging his whole hind end. He was wiggling so hard, he couldn't even keep his big, clunky paws on the ground. Fact was, I thought he was going to shake himself clear apart.

I rubbed my cheek on Luigi's leg, then rubbed on Willy's leg. Luigi's deep, rumbling laugh rolled like thunder.

"Dumb Luigi. Him think big dog chase kitty cat. But kitty cat have new friend." He rubbed behind my ears. "You bring puppy dog to eat at Luigi's." He frowned, then gave a little shrug. "Maybe, pretty *big* puppy, but you two friend. Bring for Luigi to meet, right?"

"Right. You got it." I arched my back so he could get at that good spot between my shoulder blades. "This is Willy. Willy, this is my friend Luigi. He's the guy I been telling you about. The one who fixes—"

"You been telling friend about Luigi's very good spaghetti and meatballs?" Luigi interrupted. "I cook up fresh, today. Luigi go get bowl for you." He stood and looked down at Willy. "Fix *big* bowl for friend."

Willy flinched when Luigi picked up the skillet. But he didn't run away. In a moment Luigi came back. He put a small bowl in front of me. He set an enormous bowl down for Willy. It felt good to hear his laugh and feel how proud he was when Willy and I dug in.

"I'm gonna blow up!"

"Me, too!" I licked my paw and kept working on my whiskers. They were almost straight now. Still a couple of crinkles in about three of them, but they were mostly back to normal.

Willy lay flat on his back in front of his house. With his feet lopped in the air, his tummy stuck up almost as high as his chest. He wriggled and twisted, scratching his back on the grass. As much as he ate, it wouldn't surprise me if he couldn't even turn himself back over.

"You need to learn how to eat Italian."

"Huh?"

"You got to slow down. Take it one bite at a

time," I explained. "Italian food has to be savored and enjoyed."

"I did enjoy it. It was the best stuff I ever ate."

"You didn't eat the first bowl—you inhaled it. I mean, one second Luigi put it down. The next second it was gone!"

Willy flopped to his side. "I still enjoyed it. I think we ought to go back tomorrow."

I shook my head. "Don't want to overdo it. About twice a week is plenty. More than that and Luigi might get tired of us."

Willy started wriggling and rubbing his side on the grass. He used his paws to drag himself. After he scratched and itched in a complete circle, he stopped to face me again.

"So, what are we gonna do tomorrow?"

I started to answer. Ever so slowly my whiskers began to droop.

CHAPTER 10

So, what are we gonna do?"

Willy asked the very same thing when I came to his house the next morning. I still didn't have an answer. Half the night I'd spent prowling around the house. I tried to think of stuff to do—but what can you do with a dog?

"I thought we'd just lay around and rest today."

His big, floppy jowls drooped low. Then his nose crinkled up.

"That's no fun," he complained. "I like getting out. You're a cat. You don't know what it's like being a dog—being stuck in a pen all day—not being able to climb out or go explore or just go for a walk. Now that we figured out how to get through the gate, I don't want to waste a minute of it."

I licked a paw and combed the hair between my ears. "I'm really kind of tired. Why don't we just relax."

"Well, what did you and your friends used to do?" Willy asked. "Maybe we could do that."

"Nothing much." I shrugged my fur.

"You guys just didn't sit around all day. What did you do?"

"Not much. Really."

"Tell me. Please."

"There's nothing to tell," I lied. "Other than going to Luigi's twice a week, we really didn't do hardly anything."

Frowning, Willy studied me a moment or two. Then kind of a sly smile rippled across his big face.

"I know you did something. Tell me about it." He patted the floor beside him with a paw. "Come on . . ." He paused. ". . . up Chuck."

Suddenly my tail shot straight in the air. Willy's sly smile stretched clear across his face. My whiskers sprang out.

"You did that on purpose, didn't you?"

"What?" He arched his eyebrows and tried to look innocent. Rottweilers aren't very good liars. The way he fought to keep the smile off his face was a dead giveaway.

"You did do it on purpose," I hissed. Back arched and tail fuzzed, I took a couple of sideways bounces toward him. "Don't do that, Willy. You know how much it upsets me."

He fought harder to keep the smile off his face.

"I was just teasin'. Don't get so fuzzed . . . up, Chuck."

My back was arched so high that my back paws almost touched my front ones. I bounced closer.

"Willy! So help me . . ."

Suddenly the smile left his big, ugly face. "All right. I'll quit teasing. But you quit lying. Tell me what you and your friends used to do."

"You really want to know?" I glared at him through tight eyes.

"Yes. I really want to know."

"You *really* want to know?"

"I *really* want to know."

"All right! Fine! You really want to know, I'll tell you. We climbed trees. That sound like fun?" I didn't give him time to answer. "Sometimes we chaced mice in the empty field behind my house. That sound like something you'd like to do? But mostly . . ." I took a deep breath. It was hard for me to say—but I was really mad. "Mostly, we teased dogs! We climbed up on the fence at the football field and called them names. We made fun of the way they looked. We laughed at them and told them how dumb dogs are. There! Now you know."

My tail hung clear to the ground. I turned away,

unable to look him in the eye. Willy was my friend. Willy was also a dog. I didn't want to tell him about all the mean things we did to his kind. It was my darned temper. Why couldn't I control myself? Why did I always let it get the best of me? Why did I let my temper make me say and do things I shouldn't? Now . . . now it was too late. I wasn't even gentle or kind about telling him—I just blurted it out. Now Willy could never forgive me. Now we could never be friends. Maybe dogs and cats just weren't meant to be . . .

Willy nudged me with his nose. It was a gentle nudge, but he was so big, it almost rolled me. I turned to look at him.

A tender smile cocked his big, ugly head to the side.

"It's okay," he said. "You were young, then. You didn't know any better. We didn't even know each other then. It's okay. Really."

A gulping sound came out of my throat.

"I'm sorry."

"Why?" He shrugged his ears. "I mean, if Tuffy hadn't been such a good cat and hadn't raised me like she did . . . well . . . who knows, I might have turned out like Rocky. I mean, I might have chased cats and tried to eat them and stuff. But we're friends now. Right? All that stuff is behind us. I'm not any good at climbing trees. Making fun of dogs doesn't sound like much fun, either. Besides, as much as I ate at Luigi's yesterday, I'd probably break the fence down. But we can still find stuff to do together. We're friends. Friends can find things to do that both of us can enjoy. Come on."

I followed Willy to the big, double wooden gate. He shoved his nose through the crack and forced it open. Then he pushed his head through. Struggling, he got his shoulders, waist, and hips past the opening. One step before his rump cleared the gate, he stopped.

"Come on. I'll hold the gate for you."

"Where are we going?" I asked.

"Let's go chase the mice. If that doesn't work, we can see what's on the other side of the empty field."

I stopped—right in the middle of the gate.

"Oh, we can't go there!"

"Why not?"

"Farmer McVee's place is on the other side of the empty field. There's monsters who live there. They're huge—even bigger than you are. All they know how to say is 'Moo.' And they got teeth growing out of the tops of their heads. They're big and mean and horrible and scary and—"

'They say moo and have teeth growing out of their heads." Willy laughed. Then he spun around to face me.

Only trouble . . . when Willy turned around, his rump moved. I was still in the opening when the gate slammed shut.

CHAPTER 11

Willy, I really like you. Okay?"

He didn't answer. He just stood there with his head down.

"I mean, you're the nicest friend I ever had," I went on. "You're understanding and sweet and fun to be with. I think the world of you. Okay?"

His head ducked even lower.

"But Willy?"

A soft, brown eye peeked up at me.

"I really need you to listen to me this time. Are you listening Willy?"

"Yes, Chuck."

"You sure?"

"Yes, Chuck."

"DO NOT!!!" I roared. "Never, Never, NEVER!!! Don't EVER throw me in your water bowl— AGAIN!"

"But when the gate clunked you on the head—"

"No *buts*," I hissed. "I know what happened when the gate hit me. But I don't care. If I'm knocked out—just let me lie there. If I'm dead—just let me lie there. But whatever you do . . . don't throw me in the water bowl! I'm gonna be the first cat in history to have webbed feet if you keep this up."

With my tongue I squeezed more water from the fur on my left side. It dripped to the ground, gathered with the water that had already dropped off of me and made a mud puddle at my feet.

"But you keep getting knocked out."

"I never got knocked out in my whole life! Not even once—until I started hanging around with you!"

Willy's head hung so low, his nose touched the ground.

"I'm sorry," he whimpered.

Gently I touched the knot on my head. I yanked my paw away. It still hurt. Even more tenderly, I felt it again. It was starting to swell.

"Why did you start laughing at me and let go of the gate, anyway?"

Willy's enormous shoulders gave a little shrug.

"The way you were describing cows, I couldn't help but get tickled. I didn't mean to move and let the gate bang you in the head, though."

I frowned. "What's cows?"

Willy fought to keep the smile off his face. "They're those big, hairy, frightening *monsters*, with teeth growing out of their heads."

I slurped more water from my fur and glared at him.

"It's not funny," I scolded. "They *are* big. They're huge! And they *do have* teeth growing out of their heads. I've seen them."

"Those aren't teeth." Willy shook his head. "They're horns."

"What are horns."

"The things sticking out of the tops of their heads."

"But what *are* those things?"

"Horns."

"I know that, but what are horns?"

"They're the things that stick out of the tops of cows' heads."

My eyes rolled. Trying to talk with a Rotten Willy was like trying to talk with a . . . with a . . . dog. The whole conservation was just going round and round in circles.

"They're really gentle," Willy insisted. "They won't eat you. All they eat is grass. They even run from you if you bark at them. Come on. I'll show you."

I followed him toward the gate. I could just see me—a cat—barking at those big, woolly monsters. What was that dumb dog thinking? When Willy got to the gate, he leaned to stick his nose in the crack. Quickly I darted in front of him.

"Hold it. Let me go first, okay?"

Willy gave one of his sheepish smiles.

"Oh, yeah. Sure. Good idea."

Willy was probably one of the greatest cow chasers in the world. Like he said, the beasts were gentle and did nothing but munch grass. But when he barked and ran toward them, their heads shot straight in the air on one end and their tails shot straight in the air on the other. They screamed "MOO" and took off. Their ropelike tails had little tufts of hair on the end. They looked like flags as they lifted them in the air and raced away. They were so big and heavy, their feet shook the ground as they ran. Willy was hot on their heels.

But chasing cows was something we simply couldn't do, together. It didn't take a genius to figure out that as big as they were—even if they were gentle—one false move and I would end up squashed like a bug. I watched from a tree until Willy came to join me. He didn't chase them for very long. That was because he said the people animals got all bent out of shape if they saw dogs chasing their cow animals.

Next we tried the mice.

I was probably one of the greatest mousers in the world. Willy wasn't too hot. He could smell where

they had been and managed to chase one into a hole. I showed him how to pounce. Only when he tried it, there was no mouse left to play with. The thing was smushed flat. It's no fun to chase mice if you can't play with them after you catch them. Chasing cows was something we simply couldn't do together. So was chasing mice.

The sun was hanging low in the blue sky. It was almost time for Willy's people to get home from their work place. It wouldn't do for them to see how we got in and out of Willy's yard. People animals are not very understanding. If they knew we were out running around and having a good time, they'd fix the gate so we couldn't leave.

Willy trotted ahead of me. He looked back, over his big shoulder.

"What say we go to Luigi's tomorrow? We could get there around noon, eat, then go check out that busy street."

"I don't like the busy street," I told him. "It's scary and dangerous."

"Not if you know how to work the light." He grinned over his shoulder. "My David taught me how to cross big streets. We'll have to check it out and see if it has one of those talkie-lights. If it does, I'll teach you how to get across."

"What's a talkie-light?"

"Well, it's this light on a pole. It has boxes underneath that talk. If you watch them . . ."

I stopped listening to him. That was because, just ahead of us, I saw a black-and-white kitty cat. I'd seen it once before, but I hadn't tried to make friends. That was because, although it looked like a kitty cat, it had a bushy tail and it smelled kind of funny. Willy was looking over his shoulder, talking to me and not paying any attention to where he was going.

"Hey, watch where you're walking. You're gonna run into that black kitty cat with the white stripe."

Willy's eyes flashed. He yanked his head around.

"That's no kitty cat," he yelped. "That's a . . ."

CHAPTER 12

Skunk?"

"Skunk!"

When Willy answered and nodded his head, white foam slobbers flew everywhere. Again, he dropped on the ground to roll. He rolled and rubbed against the grass. He pushed the side of his face into the dirt and scraped and scrubbed.

Even standing upwind, the smell was horrible. It made my eyes hurt. Willy coughed and blinked. He sputtered and gagged. He used a big paw to rub at his swollen eyes.

"Why didn't you warn me sooner?" He sneezed.

"I didn't see him. You *are* kind of big. It's hard to see around you. As soon as I spotted him I told you."

He stood and shook himself. Then reeling and

pitching, he flopped back on the ground—still trying to rub the horrible stuff off.

The smell was totally yucky. The little black
kitty with the white stripe didn't give us any warning. He just turned around, lifted his tail and
WHAM!

The spray hit Willy right square in the face. A
fine mist filled the air. The little droplets left their
foul stench on everything they touched. When I
licked my fur, it put a nasty taste in my mouth.
How we made it home, I'm still not sure. Willy
couldn't see. I walked ahead of him, meowing every
step of the way so he could follow the sound of my
voice. He squeezed through the gate just as we
heard the sound of the Mama's car drive up in front
of the house. Once Willy was safely in his yard, I
headed home. But even from my back porch, I
could hear the Mama's squeal when she opened the
door to feed him. When the Daddy got home, I
could hear both of them complaining about the way
Willy smelled. They spent a long time checking the
fence for a hole or something where the skunk
might have gotten into their yard.

At my house the reaction was pretty much the
same. When the Mama opened the door to let me
in, she gagged and held her nose with her paw.
Then she kicked me out! She didn't even pick me
up—she just shoved me with her foot until I went.

She set my food bowl on the back porch and slammed the door in my face.

The next day even Luigi treated us like outcasts. He didn't come to the door when I jumped on the screen to tell him we were there. I could hear pots and pans clattering around, then suddenly everything got quiet.

"Dennis," Luigi's voice called. "There's a skunk outside. Close a the door! Quick! Close a the door before all our customers run away."

"We're not skunks," I meowed. "It's us. Chuck and Willy."

The young man in the white apron didn't listen. He just sneered down his snout at us and slammed the door.

After three days I didn't think I smelled so bad. But the Mama wouldn't let me in the house for a whole week. Willy got hit with more of the spray than I did. It was almost two weeks before I could stand to go in his doghouse. Every morning Willy came out and rubbed himself in the grass. Then he'd trot over to where I was and ask if the smell was gone. Horrible as the stench was, I guess a fella gets used to it. One day I sniffed and smiled. "Let's go eat." Only when we got to Luigi's, the Dennis boy came to the back door. He sniffed, frowned at us, and slammed the door again. Three weeks was a long time to go without spaghetti and meatballs.

"Hey, how's a my boys dis morning. Long time, no see." Luigi smiled, then sniffed the air. "You two no chasea da skunks no more. Good. You hungry for Luigi's good spaghetti and meatballs?"

"You bet!" Willy wagged his tail. I hopped down from the screen before Luigi flung it opened and mangled my whiskers.

"We weren't chasing the skunk," I explained. "We just sort of stumbled onto him and . . ."

Like always, Luigi didn't listen. He scurried inside his restaurant and brought back a big bowl for Willy and a smaller one for me. When he put them down, he wiped the meat sauce on his apron. Willy practically leaped for his bowl. It's a wonder he didn't get Luigi's fingers.

"Remember," I told him. "You got to eat Italian slow. Savor every bite."

Willy just couldn't help himself. He gobbled spaghetti and meatballs as fast as he could. Luigi only laughed. He laced his thumbs in the straps of his apron and rocked back on his heels. His loud, rumbling laugh made me feel good.

"Gots lots of peoples inside today." He chuckled. "Gots to go feed them. You boys be good. Not chase no more skunks—okay?" He left us to finish our meal.

*   *   *

After we ate, Willy wanted to go to the busy street. I didn't. No matter how much I wanted to explore on the other side of the road, or how much confidence I had that Willy really did know how to get across—I simply didn't want to go. Every time I looked at the busy street, or so much as thought about it, the vision of Louie crept into my head. I could still see him, lying still and cold in the road.

"Let's go back to your house," I suggested. "We could chase mice in the field. You need to practice your pouncing. Maybe I could teach you how to land on their tails, instead of flattening them and—"

"Come on, Chuck," he called over his shoulder. "We don't have to cross if you don't want to. Let's just go check it out."

Car things zoomed and whizzed and roared past. There were so many of them and they were so thick, I couldn't even see the other side of the street.

At the corner Willy sat on his stub tail and smiled at me.

"It's a talkie-light, all right. See?"

He pointed with his nose. There were three lights on top of the pole. When the green light was on, car things rushed beside us. When the yellow light came on, they rushed faster. But when the red light came on, they stopped and the cars in front of us rushed past. I watched it a long time. Still . . .

"I didn't hear it say anything," I admitted finally.

Willy sighed. "Don't look at the round lights. Look at the square lights underneath."

I frowned. Squinted my sharp eyes.

In a square box under the round lights were some red marks:

$$\textbf{D - O - N - ' - T}$$
$$\textbf{W - A - L - K}$$

I watched for a long time, only they didn't do anything.

"It's still not talking," I told him.

"Yeah, it is," Willy said. "It's people talk. But the white letters don't come on. I must be forgetting something. But it's a talkie-light."

I cocked my head and looked at him out of one eye.

"Okay. If it's a talkie-light, what does it say?"

Willy smiled. "See those red marks?"

"Yeah."

"The ones that look like

$$\textbf{D - O - N - ' - T}$$
$$\textbf{W - A - L - K}$$

"They say, 'Stay, Willy. Stay!' Only, there's a white light with marks underneath it. W - A - L - K says, 'Come on, Willy. Let's go.' "

"I don't see the white marks."

Willy nodded. "My David used to do something to make the white marks come on. Only I can't remember . . . Oh, yeah! We got to push the button."

CHAPTER 13

Loretta? Did you see that?" An old man people yelled from inside one of the car things.

"See what?" a woman people asked.

"That cat! He was standing on that big dog's head and pushing the button for the crosswalk."

"Oh, you crazy old coot," her voice squawked. "You're blind as a bat. You must be losing your mind. A cat standing on a dog's head. That's the most ridiculous thing I've ever . . ."

I couldn't hear the rest of what they said. As their car thing moved away, their voices were flooded out by all the other rushing car things. I hopped down from Willy's head and stood beside him.

In a moment all the car things stopped.

"See?" Willy's smile stretched from ear to ear. "It's just like My David said: W - A - L - K says, 'Come on, Willy. Let's go.' "

"You're right," I agreed. "It's worked the same way every time."

"So, are you ready to cross?"

"I'm ready."

Willy's paw was too big to fit inside the metal thing on the pole. He stood with his nose against it. I hopped on his back. Quickly I walked to the top of his head and stuck my paw on the button. The car things zoomed and whizzed. Then the 'Let's go, Willy' light came on and they stopped.

We trotted across the street, while all the car things waited for us.

"You can read, Willy."

Confused, he looked at me a moment. Then a gentle smile came. "You know, I never thought of it that way. You're right, Chuck. I *can* read!" His little stub tail wagged his whole rear end.

Willy didn't want to go to the mall. He said that there were too many cars and they came flying from all different directions. So we went where the houses were. There were all sorts of smells. In one of the houses someone was cooking bread. In another, peoples were laughing and talking. A dog rushed to a fence and barked at us as we passed. Willy sniffed. He told me that the bird dog was nice. He was only barking because he didn't know us and was protecting his property. In the middle of the block a cat saw us coming. He scurried up a tree before I could even say hello.

The cat stopped on a lower branch. Willy waited on the sidewalk while I went over and put my paws on the tree trunk.

"Hi. My name's Chuck," I purred at the cat. "We live on the other side of the busy street. My friend and I are exploring. We're trying to find new friends. Would you like to be . . ."

I never got to finish asking if he wanted to be our friend. Right in the middle of what I was saying, a dog came tearing from the front porch of a house. His bark was a high-pitched yap. It hurt my ears and made me blink.

"Get out of my yard!" he snarled. "I'm gonna eat you up. I'm gonna get you!"

My tail fuzzed. He wasn't a big dog. He wasn't little, either. He was a black-and-white Collie, only smaller than most Collies I had seen. I guess he was what was called a Miniature Collie—and he was as hyper as could be. He came tearing right for me. It took me so much by surprise that my feet wouldn't move. My claws wouldn't come out to climb the tree. I just stood there, frozen like an idiot.

Suddenly Willy was beside me. He looked at the Collie and bared his teeth.

"Stop!" he ordered. "Don't hurt my friend."

"I'm gonna get that cat. I'm gonna chew him up and . . ."

The Collie stopped dead in his tracks. He looked

Willy up and down. His mouth kind of flopped open when he saw how big Willy was. Then . . .

He let out a squeal, like Willy had taken a bite out of him or something. He wheeled around. He ran. Not in a straight line, like most dogs. He spun round and round in circles as he raced back to his house. He never stopped whining, squealing, and spinning all the way to his porch.

A woman flung the door open. She reached down and picked up the dog and hugged him.

"Oh, poor baby," she cooed. "Did the big, bad dog hurt my little BooBoo?" Still clutching the noisy mutt to her and whispering goo-goo, baby-stuff in his ear, she glared at Willy. "Bad dog! Bad dog! You leave my BooBoo alone. Get out of here!"

Willy smiled and wagged his tail.

"I didn't touch him!" Willy whimpered. "Honest. I just told him not to hurt my friend. . . ."

"You evil, terrible monster. You get out of here, right this minute!"

"Help me! Help me!" the cat began to cry from up in the tree. "That big, black beast is going to eat me. Somebody help me!"

"He's not a beast," I hissed. "He's a Rotten . . . I mean a Rottweiler. His name is Willy. He's my friend. He's really nice and sweet and—"

"Help me! Don't let the monster eat me! Help! Help! Help!"

No matter how I tried to explain, the cat

wouldn't shut up. He just kept yelling. A woman came to the porch of the house next door. "I'll call the pound!" she shouted. The woman hugging Boo-Boo yelled back to her: "Hurry."

"What's the pound?" I asked.

"Don't know," Willy answered. "Whatever it is, she's gonna call it."

It didn't take a genius to tell we weren't wanted. Willy and I trotted down the street. We could find other cats and dogs who were nicer. We could find someone who wanted to be our friends.

In the middle of the next block Willy started sniffing the air. He trotted down an alley and put his front paws on a trash can.

"Man, something in here smells really yummy."

"I can't believe you're hungry," I said. "I'm still so full from Luigi's, I'm about to bust. After all we had for lunch, surely you're not going to—"

The roar of a car thing cut my question short. I looked up. A white car thing whizzed toward us. It had a box on the back and a blue light on top. It was coming really fast. Quickly I darted under the trash holder. Willy let go of the trash can and leaned against the fence so it could pass.

Only it didn't go past us. It stopped. A man people in a brown uniform, with a little, shiny star pinned to his shirt, hopped out. From the side of the car thing, he took a long pole. It had a loop of wire or rope on the end of it. He started toward Willy.

"Here, puppy. Come here, boy," he coaxed. He held his hand out like he was offering Willy some food or something. But his hand was empty. Then glancing down, he spotted me. His big paw reached out. It barely touched my ear before I scrunched farther under the trash can holder. "Stinkin' cat," he mumbled to himself. "I'll get you later." He turned back to Willy. "Nice puppy. Come on."

Friendly as always, Willy's tail started to wag. He moved toward the man.

"Wait, Willy," I whispered. "Something's wrong. Don't come over here."

Suddenly the man people thrust the pole. The loop went around Willy's head. Then the man yanked! The rope drew tight around my friend's throat. Willy's eyes flashed as big around as my head. He tried to jump back. Run.

"I can't breathe," he gasped. "He's choking me. It's killing me. Help!"

The man people with the brown uniform laughed. He dragged Willy toward the back of his car thing. There were boxes there. Cages with bars and holes.

"Help me, Chuck," Willy pleaded.

I poked my head from under the trash can.

"What can I do, Willy? I'm just a kitty cat. All I

know how to do is purr and meow. I only know how to chase mice and—"

"Come on, big boy," the man people groaned. "Soon as you're locked up, I'll get your buddy over there."

Legs locked and paws plowing up the dirt, Willy tried to stop. He was big and strong, but no match for the man people.

"Run, Chuck!" Willy gagged. "Don't let him get you, too. There's nothing you can do. Run!"

Willy was right. Now was my chance!

While the man was busy, fighting with Willy, I could make a break for it. I could get away. I could find some place safe to hide. Late at night, when there were not many cars on the busy street, I could get back to my home—to my family.

I darted from my hiding place and ran.

No matter how I wanted to help my friend, Willy was right. There was nothing I could do. I was just a kitty cat. All we're good for is purring and meowing and chasing mice and . . .

CHAPTER 14

I had only bounded a few strides when my legs locked up. Still choking Willy with the rope, the man bent over. He put his free hand under my friend's chest and began to lift him toward the cage. Before I even stopped sliding, I spun around and charged.

Bent over with his back to me, the man people was the perfect target. He never saw me coming. I leaped.

Claws out, I sailed through the air. I latched on to the man's leg and started to climb.

"YOWIEEEE!" he screamed.

I kept climbing. The man people began jumping around. He flailed his arms. He danced about. He tried to grab me with his big paws. I went right up his leg, past his bottom, and up his back. He couldn't reach me.

"OUCH!"

I kept climbing. I went clear to the very top. There, balled up on his head, I hung on for dear life.

For a second or two he hopped and danced around in circles. He screamed and bounced. Then enormous paws wrapped about me and ripped me from my perch. Suddenly I was flying through the air. Tail and back spinning, I landed on my feet. I was on top of the car thing.

In a flash I scurried across the box, slid down the windshield, and hopped to the ground. I hid underneath.

Willy was there. His paws dug at the rope around his neck. Frightened eyes flashed at me. He was almost loose. Still, he needed more time.

Before the man people could find me, I darted from the car thing and hid under the trash cans. There, I watched as he rubbed his leg with his paw. He touched it to his head, then stared down at it for a long time to see if there was any blood. Then his big paws made fists. He bent over to look under the car thing.

It was too much to pass up.

Well . . . Willy needed more time to get the rope loose. And . . . well . . . the man people was all bent over, trying to see under the car thing. And . . . well . . . the way his big, fat rump stuck up in the air, right in front of the trash can where I was hiding . . . well . . .

"YOWIEEEEEE!"

My sharp claws clung to his leg. My sharp teeth crunched as they sank through his brown pants and into his fat bottom.

"OUCH! OUCH! OUCH!"

A big paw clunked me upside the head. Another paw whacked me from the other direction. He started running around in circles. In less than a second he was spinning—whizzing faster and faster until I could hardly hold on. All four paws gripped as hard as I could. Suddenly my hind feet let go. Stretched out, I still clung to him with my front claws and my teeth.

He whirled faster. The force was too much. I lost my grip with my front paws. Level with the ground, I hung on with nothing but my teeth. Round and round—tail and body stretched out straight—listening to him squeal as he spun faster and faster. At last my teeth finally slipped from their grip on his fat bottom.

I felt myself sail through the air. I slammed against the fence and slid to the ground. Shaking my head, I blinked a couple of times. I scrambled to my feet. Blinked again and opened my eyes.

Willy was beside me. He nudged me with his big snout.

"I'm loose! Come on, let's get out of here!"

We flew down the alley. Behind us, I could hear

the man people screaming and shouting nasty words at us. We ran harder.

Through the alley, across a yard, up a street, and down another street. I was still running as hard as I could when we reached the busy road with all the cars. Still at full speed, I crouched to leap from the curb.

Only, I didn't go anywhere.

Something stopped me. Something stomped on my tail!

It hurt. It pinned my tail to the ground. Fact was, it almost yanked it clear out. I flinched from the pain. Claws out, I turned to attack whatever held me.

It was Willy's big paw.

"The light," he urged.

A car thing whizzed past, just inches from my nose. The wind from it ruffled my fur.

"The light," Willy repeated. "Work the light. Quick! Before he finds us. It's the only way we can get across."

In the blink of an eye I leaped to his back. I raced to his head and swatted the little black button as hard as I could.

"There they are again, Loretta," a voice called from one of the car things.

"What?" a woman people squawked.

"That crazy cat. The one over there on the dog's head."

I leaped down. The cars began to stop.

"What cat? Soon as we get home, I'm calling the doctor, Charlie. You're losin' your marbles. . . ."

Once across the busy street, we raced down the sidewalk. We heard a car coming, so we hid beside a house. When it was gone, we took the alley to Willy's. Once certain that no one was watching, we slipped through the gate and hid in Willy's doghouse.

Still panting and out of breath, we watched and listened for a long, long time. Finally certain that the man in the white car thing with the blue light hadn't followed us, we began to relax.

Willy nudged me with his nose.

"That was the bravest thing I ever saw," he said with a sigh. "You're a regular hero."

My lip curled when I tilted my head to look at him.

"Hero? Me?"

"Hero!" He nodded so hard that his big, loose jowls flopped. "The way you jumped that guy so I could get loose . . . I still can't believe it! He could have caught you. He could have locked you in a cage. You had the chance to get away, but you came back to help me. That's what I call brave. A hero!"

I crossed my paws and laid my head on them.

"I'm no hero, Willy." I sighed. "I was scared. I wanted to run away."

"But you didn't. You came back. You saved me."

"I didn't want him to get me," I admitted. "But I didn't want him to get you, either. But I'm no hero."

"You're my hero." Willy kissed me with his enormous, sloppy tongue. "How did you know what to do?"

My whiskers twitched.

"I don't know. I was trying to think what I could do if I was big, like you. Maybe I could bite him or knock him down or something. But I'm not big like you. I'm just a little kitty cat. And . . . well . . . I kept trying to think what a little, puny, kitty cat could do. And . . ."

"And?" he urged.

I looked at my friend a moment and smiled.

"What *can* kitty cats do?" I asked him.

Willy frowned. He looked at me, and slowly a smile came to his big, ugly face.

"Well, cats can meow. Cats can purr." He kind of nibbled on his bottom lip. "They can smell funny—like a cat. They can hiss and spit. Some of them get all fuzzed up when you call them by their nickname. They can catch mice. And . . ." He stopped, kind of nibbling at the other side of his lip.

"And?" I nudged him with my paw.

A sly smile curled his lips.

"And they can climb trees. Right?"

I took a deep breath and sighed.

"Right. I think it was the brown pants," I confessed. "If the guy had on blue pants or shorts—I might never have thought of it. But brown pants . . . long legs . . . it kind of reminded me of a tree trunk. And when cats are scared—we climb a tree. It's the first thing that comes to our mind."

"I'm glad you were there," Willy said. "I'm glad you were there for me today. I'm glad you're my friend, Chuck."

He kissed me again with that huge tongue.

Getting kissed by a dog is kind of revolting. Dog kisses are wet and sloppy. Besides . . . well . . . dogs smell like dogs.

His big head made a thud sound when he flopped it down to take a nap. I snuggled up close to him and nestled my head against his tummy.

So he was a dog. So what?

I peeked up at the gigantic beast beside me.

"I'm glad you're my friend, too, Willy."

ABOUT THE AUTHOR

BILL WALLACE was a principal and physical education teacher at an elementary school in Chickasha, Oklahoma, for ten years. Recently, he has spent much of his spare time assisting his wife in coaching a girls' soccer team. When Bill's not busy on the soccer field, he spends time with his family, cares for his five dogs, three cats, and two horses, lectures at schools around the country, answers mail from his readers, and of course, works on his books. Bill Wallace's novels have won nineteen state awards and made the master lists in twenty-four states.